Seasonal Dreamer

Home Is In My Suitcase

By

Jermaine Andre Howard

Author: Jermaine Andre Howard

ISBN: 978-1-972225-10-3

Library of Congress Control Number: 2026906833

Printed in the United States of America.

For permissions, bulk purchases, or special edition inquiries, please contact the author.

Dedication

This book is dedicated to all the wonderful people I have met along the way, in all the restaurants and resorts I have had the pleasure to work in. The H2B journey has shaped me into the man I am today.

I would also like to dedicate this book to my wife, Renae, and my children, Carick and Zeiandre, who were with me and still with me through my journey—a warm home from a distance, also when I returned home.

Acknowledgment

First and foremost, I give thanks to God for the strength, protection, and guidance throughout my journey. Without faith, perseverance, and hope, this story would never have been written.

I want to express my deepest gratitude to my family for their unconditional love, encouragement, and sacrifices. Even when distance separated us, your support remained my motivation to keep pushing forward and chasing my dreams. This book is a reflection of the strength you helped build within me.

To my wife, Renae, thank you for always standing beside me, believing in me, and supporting my dreams even during the most challenging times. Your love, patience, and encouragement kept me grounded and focused when the journey felt overwhelming. You have been my emotional anchor and my constant source of strength.

I would also like to give special thanks to Velecia, the woman who helped make this journey begin and who kept me emotionally strong along the way. Your encouragement, belief in my potential, and support played a major role in shaping my path. Your influence will always be a meaningful part of my story.

To my friends and fellow H-2B workers, thank you for sharing this journey with me. The long hours, sleepless nights, laughter, struggles, and shared dreams created bonds that will last a lifetime. Your stories, resilience, and determination inspired many of the moments captured in this book.

I would also like to thank the Pelican Bay community and my coworkers at Marker 36. You played an important role in my professional growth and helped shape me into the person and server I am today. The lessons, challenges, and opportunities you provided helped me discover my passion for hospitality and service.

To every mentor, manager, and guest who believed in me, encouraged me, and trusted my service, thank you for helping me grow in confidence and skill. Each interaction helped shape my journey in ways you may never realize.

Finally, I thank every reader who takes the time to experience my story. I hope my journey reminds you that dreams often come with sacrifice, courage, and resilience. No matter where you come from, your journey matters, and your dreams are valid.

With gratitude,

Jermaine Andre Howard

Contents

Page Blank Intentionally

Prologue

Home is not something an H-2B worker leaves behind. It becomes something we learn to carry.

Every season begins almost the same way—with a visa approval, a carefully packed suitcase, and a goodbye that never feels any easier, no matter how many times you've done it before. The suitcase holds uniforms, worn work boots, documents folded and unfolded so many times the ink begins to fade, and a few personal items that remind us who we were before the job title replaced our names.

What it cannot hold are the things that matter most—family dinners missed, birthdays celebrated through a phone screen, children growing taller in photos instead of in our arms, and the quiet ache of knowing life is moving forward without us.

This journey is built on temporary permission and permanent sacrifice. We arrive with contracts in hand, return dates already decided, and rules that quietly define how long we are allowed to exist in someone else's country. We work hard because failure is never just personal. Too many people back home depend on every hour we clock in, every paycheck we send, every promise we made before boarding that plane.

Home in My Suitcase tells the truth about life inside the H-2B program, the early mornings that start before the sun, the shared housing where strangers become survival partners, the pressure to perform, and the silent strength it takes to keep smiling through exhaustion. It speaks about dignity earned through labor, resilience shaped in unfamiliar places, and the emotional cost carried by workers who are essential to the economy yet treated as temporary in status.

This book is for the seasonal workers who cross borders with hope stitched into their pockets. For the families who wait with patience and prayer. For the dreams that are postponed—but never abandoned.

I didn't travel for adventure. I didn't leave for comfort.

I traveled to provide. I traveled to survive.

And in every place I worked, lived, and waited, I carried my home with me—folded carefully between clothes and documents, packed tightly inside a suitcase, ready to reopen when the season ended.

This is my H-2B journey. This is *Home in My Suitcase.*

Chapter 1: Arrival and First Impressions

Every journey to a new land begins with a single step - a step away from everything familiar, everything comfortable, everything known. For thousands of workers who leave their home countries each year under the H2B visa program, that step is both an act of courage and an act of faith. It is a belief that sacrifice today will yield a better tomorrow, that distance from loved ones will somehow translate into security for those same loved ones, that the American Dream, however elusive, however demanding, is still worth chasing.

This is a story of one such journey: of leaving behind a pregnant wife and a life just beginning, of arriving in a world of wealth and luxury as an outsider looking in, and of learning that survival in America requires not just hard work, but resilience, adaptation, and an unwavering determination to keep moving forward no matter how heavy the burden becomes.

In 2016, I got married to my beautiful wife in July. My life was about to change in ways I couldn't have imagined. Not long after our wedding, my mother called to tell me that a friend of mine wanted to speak with me. When I called her back the following week, she told me about a job proposal; something called the H2B program, where you could come to America, work for a period of time, then return to your home country. But there was more: you could also extend for three years, staying in the United States and working, transitioning from job to job.

I had just gotten married. My wife was pregnant with our son. This was a moment when I should have been home, building our life together, preparing for fatherhood. But the opportunity felt too significant to ignore. I wanted to provide a better future for my wife and my unborn son. So I decided to accept the proposal.

My friend came to Jamaica for a job fair, and I went to the interview. I felt confident; she was the one who had offered me the proposal in the first place, so I was 100% sure I would get the job. But there was one problem: I had never done this type of work before. Never in my life had I been a server or worked in the hospitality industry. Still, I went through with it. I signed up with the agent, went to the embassy, and got my visa approved for six months to work at Pelican Bay Foundation in Naples, Florida.

This was a very hard decision; leaving my pregnant wife to come to America. It felt odd, almost wrong, but I told myself it was for our future.

On November 2nd, 2016, I boarded an American Airlines flight. There were three of us traveling together: two girls and I, all heading to Pelican Bay. I didn't know either of them, and I had even forgotten the faces of the people I'd interviewed with at the job fair. Everything felt unfamiliar.

We landed at Miami International Airport at 10 PM. I was confused at first because everyone at the airport was speaking Spanish. I thought for a moment that I had landed in a Spanish country. I knew I was in America, but the language threw me off. Eventually, I realized there were just a lot of Spanish-speaking people living in Miami.

We met a bus outside the airport and drove for three and a half hours to reach Housing which was located at Cypress. When we finally arrived, we stood outside the apartment building for at least an hour and a half because we didn't have the access code to get inside. Eventually, another worker drove up; a Jamaican guy we called the Ants Man because he was small and black. He made some calls and helped us get inside.

I was assigned to apartment 103. The two girls I had traveled with decided to share the apartment with me, and another guy arrived a week later. It was cramped; the other guy and I shared a small room with two bunk beds, while the girls had another room. I spent six months in Pelican Bay during the first season.

The following morning, I went to HR and met Joyce, the HR manager. She welcomed us warmly, gave us goodies and coffee, and helped us with our paperwork. Then we were introduced to our managers and taken to the restaurant where we would be working for lunch.

My manager was Velicia. There was another manager, Agna, from a different restaurant who wanted me to work as a server. But at the time, I didn't know what being a server was all about. I didn't know the difference between wine and champagne in terms of service. I didn't know how to approach a table or what the steps of service were. I decided I needed to start from scratch.

I told Velicia I wanted to be a busser instead. I wanted to learn the basics: how to set a table, clear a table, run food, and understand the difference between salads, entrees, and desserts. I wanted to know all the steps of service before I tried to be a server.

They trained me on the micro machine for a few weeks. The next day, I showed up in my orange shirt, black pants, and polished black shoes, ready to work. I was assigned to train with Andrei. He trained me for four days, but at the end, he told the manager I wasn't suitable to be a server. Velicia had been trying me out to see if I could handle it, but I had already told her I wanted to be a busser. So that's what I became.

For that entire first season, I bussed tables, cleared dishes, and ran food at Marker 36. I didn't see my wife for six months. My son was born on April 18th, 2017, and I wasn't there. I didn't get to see him when he was born. All my interactions with my wife were over the phone.

The first night I arrived in America, I couldn't even talk to her. I didn't have an American phone number yet. The internet wasn't connecting on my phone; I didn't have a smartphone, just one of those old phones. I had to use roaming to call her directly, and I had to receive calls straight from her. The only other device I had was a tablet I'd borrowed from my in-laws, but I couldn't connect it to the internet right away.

I was so depressed. I was so distraught about leaving my wife back in Jamaica, knowing she was pregnant and that we had just gotten married two months before. The loneliness was crushing me inside. But I kept telling myself I was doing this for us, for our future, for the home I wanted to build for my family.

Pelican Bay Foundation was unlike anything I had ever seen. It was nestled in the midst of luxury and nature in a way I had never witnessed before. When we drove through the gates, the landscape changed completely.

Well-manicured lawns stretched out in perfect green. Palm trees lined the roads like soldiers on parade. In the distance, I could see the gleam of the Gulf of Mexico, turquoise and endless.

This wasn't what I had expected. This was an affluence as I had only seen in movies. The cars parked in front of the restaurants and clubhouses were shiny and expensive: Mercedes, BMWs, Porsches. Women in tennis whites walked by with rhinestone-studded leashes attached to small dogs. Men in polo shirts talked easily on their cell phones, their laughter echoing across the perfectly landscaped grounds.

And there I was, getting out of a shuttle with one ragged suitcase and shoes I had polished three times to hide the scratches. I felt small; smaller than I had ever felt in my life.

The staff housing was modest compared to the grandeur around it, but even modest here was better than what I had left behind. It was a plain apartment with plain white walls, plain furnishings, and a window that looked out onto a cluster of mangroves. I dropped my suitcase on the floor and sat on the edge of the bed, the springs squeaking under my weight.

The silence was deafening. I was completely alone in a way I had never been before. No family. No friends. No familiar voices to break the silence. Just me and the sound of the air conditioning struggling against the Florida heat.

I wanted to cry, but the tears wouldn't come. I just sat there, staring at my hands, wondering what I had gotten myself into.

The following morning came too soon. I had barely slept, my body still confused about what time of day it was, my mind full of anxiety about what lay ahead. I showered, put on the uniform they had sent me: black trousers, an orange button-up shirt, and black shoes, and looked at myself in the bathroom mirror.

You can do this, I told my reflection. *You didn't come all this way to fail.*

But the face staring back at me didn't look convinced.

This was my new world. Unfamiliar, overwhelming, and terrifying. But it was mine. And I was going to figure out how to survive in it.

Chapter 2: Work Life

The challenges I faced in my first season as an H2B worker were unlike anything I had experienced before. Not knowing what the food was like, interacting and serving people I didn't know, living with people I had never met, these were all obstacles I had to navigate daily.

You meet people from countries you've never even heard of. Sometimes people would tell me they were from Hungary or Romania, and while I knew these countries existed on a map, I had never really recognized them until I traveled as an H2B and met people from these places. I worked with Mexicans in my first season, lots of them. People from England came to the United States to work, just to change their lives. People from Hungary and Romania, in my second season, I worked with many of them. Cultural diversity taught me so much. We all came from different walks of life, but we met here in America to work, to make our families comfortable and happy. It was an odd feeling to experience, but also enlightening.

The alarm clock woke me up at 5:30 AM, dragging me out of a short and restless sleep. I hit it blindly, stopping the noise, and sat there for a moment staring at the ceiling. Parts of my body that weren't supposed to hurt were sore. My feet still ached from the day before. But there was no time to ease into the day. At Pelican Bay

Foundation, the morning shift began at 6:30 AM sharp, and being late was not an option.

In those first three weeks, I learned that it wasn't enough to survive simply. At the Marker 36 Restaurant, you either kept up or you were left behind.

Formally, I was a food runner, which didn't sound that complex on paper. In practice, it meant I was a crucial link in a chain that could never be broken. I carried finished dishes from the kitchen and delivered them to guests' tables at exactly the right time. Speed was important, and so was presentation; a plate that looked like a work of art coming out of the kitchen had to reach the table in the same condition.

After six months at Pelican Bay, my season ended in May. That's when another challenge emerged: finding another job. The agent reached out to us with flyers. It was very difficult for me because of my limited experience. By then, I had started developing the skills to be a front server, not just a busser, not just a food runner, but an actual server. I had developed those skills during my six months at Pelican Bay.

The agent organized a job fair in the Pelican Bay conference room, and I interviewed with several people, but I didn't get a job. So I reached out to my agent and told her I needed a job. She sent me a contract for a place. I saw a castle on the top right corner of the contract and a name at the bottom: Quinn, the lodging manager. There was a number for him and the address. I signed it and accepted because I wanted to stay in America and make more money for my family. My son had just been born, and my wife wanted me to come home, but I told her I wanted to make more money for us. I wanted our own home so my family could be comfortable.

So I went to Belhurst Castle. But before I could leave Pelican Bay, I had to stay behind for two weeks before my flight. I was the only worker left behind. When the two weeks were up, it was a Sunday. I woke up early and booked an Uber to Fort Myers Airport.

When I got to the airport and tried to check in, they told me I wasn't booked for a flight. I had my ticket, but the agent at the counter said I wasn't booked. I told her, "Here is my flight number. Here is my flight ticket, everything." I was supposed to take three flights to get to Geneva, New York, way up near Rochester.

That was one of the biggest challenges I had to face. I went back and forth with the agent at the counter, and she kept saying there was no flight. People had to step aside so others could check in. She tried to help me, but I missed the first flight. Then she tried to get me on another flight, but I missed that one, too.

Finally, I had to call CheaperAir, the flight booking agency that had arranged my ticket. They had made a mistake and canceled my flight. I had to keep calling Belhurst Castle to reach Quinn. I was so confused and nervous. I didn't know what to do. I called my manager, Velicia, and she asked if I wanted her to get me. I told her I wanted to give it a little more time.

I called my wife back in Jamaica, and she was crying. She didn't want me to get in trouble. I was distraught at the airport, confused, but I was still resilient. I wanted to extend it for my family. I wanted to extend myself. I wanted a better future. I didn't just want to do six months and go back home.

I stayed at the airport, going back and forth with CheaperAir. My manager said he would rebook the flight and talk to them because they had messed up. I spoke with another agent, a male, and he was very rude. He told me my flight was canceled and I'd have to rebook for another day. But there was a lady, I don't remember her name, who was very nice to me. She saw that I had been booked for the flight but that it had been canceled, and she helped me get on another flight.

I stayed on the phone with CheaperAir, and they rescheduled the flight for the same day. I was at the airport from six o'clock in the morning and didn't get on a flight until 12:30 PM. I traveled to New York, taking three flights total.

When I arrived in Rochester, it was very cold. That was the first time I had ever felt cold like that. It was May, but it was still cold in Rochester, New York. I stepped outside and immediately thought, "This is too cold," so I went back inside. I saw a lady waving a card with my name on it. I went out and introduced myself. She looked like a Filipino lady. She told me Quinn was supposed to pick me up, but because my flight had changed, she would take me instead.

We drove for about an hour and a half. When we reached the place, it was a home, not an apartment, but an actual house. I lived on the top floor, and I worked as a housekeeper.

At Belhurst Castle, I met Abraham, who became a close friend. He was a laundry guy, from Jordan in the Middle East. Two weeks after I arrived, I met Kiola, another Jamaican girl who came as a housekeeper as well.

This was my first housekeeping job. I couldn't get another job as a busser or server, so I accepted this housekeeping position. It was very difficult for me in the beginning. I didn't know how to clean properly or what to do. Quinn showed me and taught me what to do. I told him honestly, "Yeah, I am a hard worker, but I don't have experience in this." He trained me, and I learned. By the end of the season, I was one of their best housekeepers.

It was a very difficult road for me. I had to walk everywhere I wanted to go because I didn't understand the taxi service. I walked to Walmart, two to three miles, and walked back with my food. Then I found a closer town where I could buy things, which made life a little easier.

I worked at Belhurst Castle as a housekeeper for six months. Then, in October, Pelican Bay reached out to me for an extension. I came back to Pelican Bay, still working as a busser. I met new people, new faces, and faced new challenges.

But before I went to my next extension in Rhode Island, something wonderful happened. After 15 months, I finally got to see my wife again. I hadn't seen my son yet, just my wife. She had her 10 years American Visa so she was able to come and visit me in February 2018.

I was so excited. I asked one of my coworkers who had a van to drive me to Miami to pick her up. The delight on her face when I saw her, I was so happy. Finally, after all that time, I got to see her. She looked different because she had cut her hair from the long length she used to have down to short hair. But she was still my beautiful wife.

My wife stayed with me for four days before going back home. After that, I didn't want to spend that long again without seeing her, so I had her come back in April.

Then I extended to Rhode Island, to Block Island, where I worked as a housekeeper again. It was difficult for me because they didn't believe in me at first. They thought a guy could never be a good housekeeper. Based on the job, my manager, Joanna, thought I was a girl when she first heard about me. When they interviewed me, I didn't see her; it was the restaurant manager who interviewed me for Ballard's.

I wanted to stay there, but I was still afraid of being a front server. So I didn't accept the server job. I took the housekeeping job instead because I didn't have enough confidence yet. I think I had developed the skill to serve, but the confidence to walk up to a table, take their drink order, take their food order, and do the steps of service, I still wasn't confident enough. So I took the housekeeping job at Ballard's.

There were only six rooms, but they were big rooms. I worked with another housekeeper named Marva. Working with Marva was very difficult. She was a nice lady, but she always told management that she was better than me and could do the job alone. Still, at the end of the season, they wanted me to come back because I cleaned so well. But I didn't accept.

The challenges at Ballard's were significant. When I first arrived, it was super cold. Not just lonely, but physically cold. There was no phone connection at the time so I couldn't talk to my wife or my family back home. To get to the island, I had to take a ferry that took 30 minutes. When I landed at the Rhode Island airport in Providence, I drove for 30 minutes to the ferry station. I had to book my own taxi, book my own ferry, and go to the island. I had to find housing myself because I had a coworker who already worked there and could help me.

Manager Joanna was mad at me because she said she had been waiting for me at the ferry station and didn't see me. When they put me in the room, there was no kitchen, just a bathroom and a box with three bunk beds that could accommodate six people. They wanted to put five people in there, but we didn't like it, so we ended up with four of us. No kitchen, just a bathroom and a small box where we slept, ate, and showered. I had to share that close proximity with three other guys, and it was very difficult.

On the island, there was just one supermarket, and it was very expensive. If you took a taxi from where we lived to where we worked, it would cost $20 for a four- to eight-minute drive. The island was expensive. But when summer came, it was booming. The ferry was always packed with crowds, and the place was buzzing.

I worked my ass off. I was working on the beach as a beach boy and doing housekeeping at the same time. When summer came, I was working long hours, from 7 AM to 10 PM. It was really difficult for my family and me because I couldn't talk to them regularly. The phone service on the island was really bad.

But my experience there taught me something important: resilience, strength, confidence, and endurance will get you through anything, through any storm. That's what I took from working at Ballard's that season.

Then I came back to Pelican Bay. But this time was different, for the first time, I got to go back to Jamaica. On October 5th, I landed in Jamaica and got to see my son for the first time. He was one and a half years old, basically one year and six months. I was so happy. I was overjoyed to see the little guy, my little me, finally. I spent a month in Jamaica, then came back to Pelican Bay as a busser again.

That's where I met Andrei. He was a server, and I started learning from him and other people. He always challenged me to become a server. When he showed me his checks and how much money he was making, I was like, "Whoa, you're making a lot of money." He told me, "If you want to be on that level, you have to develop the confidence to serve."

So I started developing confidence and self-motivation. I pushed myself to the limit where I knew I could do my best and achieve what I wanted. I worked and learned from everyone. I ran out of food. I even learned to drive; I didn't know how to drive before, so I learned and got my driver's license that season.

It was like a developing season for me, where I wanted to do the final polishing of enhancing myself as a server, as a person, uplifting myself, changing my life, and becoming a better person.

Being an H2B is not an easy task. It's difficult to find jobs every season when your present job ends. But it also builds your character as a person. Everywhere you go, you get different experiences.

This was my life now. Finding work, extending, learning, growing. It wasn't glamorous. It wasn't what I had imagined when I dreamed of coming to America. But it was real. And slowly, painfully, beautifully, I was making it mine.

Chapter 3: The Weight of Distance

The silence of pre-dawn outside still gripped Pelican Bay, but within these walls, workers such as myself were already facing the day. This wasn't just any morning. This was every morning.

I was now seated on the end of the bed, with my feet on the cold floor, and for a moment I suffered myself to meditate about home. Of those faces I would never see again today or tomorrow or in many months. Of my mother and her food, of my friends laughing, and of my old streets, and of which everybody knew my name. It was not a matter of miles between this and there. It was calculated in the number of birthdays missed, the number of conversations ending in bad connections, and the number of days spent at a virtual holiday scrolling through pictures of family get-togethers I could not attend.

This is one of the H2B worker stories that is never told. The section that occurs during the silent scenes preceding the smile you give your visitor. That is the part that lives in your chest as a stone that you drag everywhere, even when you are warming tables and pouring drinks with a steady hand.

America was not the way I had expected. Yes, I had watched it in films or heard other people who had been there before, but it was a whole new experience. I spent the initial few weeks at Pelican Bay Foundation thinking that I was in a constant state of translation, not only of words, but of different ways of living. The regulations here were stern, the policies many, and the demands great. A procedure governed each process, each job was assigned a particular way, and going off the road was not only unadvisable but also would lead you to lose your post.

This was not the same rhythm of work at home. It was structured, all right, but there was flexibility, based on knowledge and common culture. In this case, I was forced to learn everything by myself—the American way of greeting guests. What to do to arrange my service to meet the expectations was yet to be known. The code of conduct was clear to everyone except me.

The period of training was exasperating. I made notes in all of them on how to hold the tray, how to approach a table, how to deal with complaints, how to accept payments, and how to talk with the kitchen. My laptop was my Bible, with scribbled notes and shapes. I used to go through it at night, attempting to memorize everything, because I was aware that the next day there would be new challenges, new procedures, new things to remember.

Another complication was the language barrier. I could speak English, but American English was not like that. The pace of speech, the jargon, the dialects-they all joined together to make me feel that I was always one step behind. I would say yes and smile, and act as if I had understood, then hurry and find out what exactly they wanted. Other colleagues were tolerant and would be ready to explain things over. Some of them were visibly expressing their frustration, as they had to repeat themselves, and their impatience helped them to remember that I was dragging the process.

The change at Pelican Bay had been a long one, but I had anticipated it. What I had not anticipated was that the hours were going to compound, times were going to pile atop one another until days became a blur of work that would carry on in a never-ending sequence, work, short sleep, and more work. Twelve-hour shifts were made for eighteen hours and then sixteen-hour shifts. Days came when I took my appearance before the daylight, and when I had to see the sun setting before the stars before I got out of the house.

The aches in my body were something I never had before. I could always feel my feet hurting even when I was sleeping. My back complained whenever I stooped to clear a table. My hands were stiff due to the fact that I was carrying heavy trays that were loaded with plates and glasses. But I couldn't slow down. There was no lack of another table to serve, another order to take, another spill to clean, another guest who had to have something.

The physical fatigue was not too hard, though. I was young, robust, and able to persevere through the pain. The mental exhaustion was what irritated me more. The tension of being on the alert to make no errors. The stress of having the knowledge that everything that was done was being judged, that my performance did not only have an impact on me, but also on all H2B workers. The pressure of hosting a representative of my entire nation in the presence of guests and colleagues who would never get a chance to encounter someone similar to me in my home country.

We would work weeks on end and have no day off during the busiest seasons. I recall a time when I was looking at my calendar, and I knew that I had been working twenty-three days in a row. Those 23 days of getting up, having to work out of sheer exhaustion, and making it to bed with just enough energy to have some food. Three weeks of smiling and serving guests, and my body was screaming to have a rest.

The homesickness, however, was the worst of it, the bit that made all the physical difficulty of it look like nothing in comparison. It sneaked up on me when I did not anticipate it. One of my breaks, when I looked at my phone and saw pictures of my relatives celebrating, and I was not there. I did it alone at night, at the time when the room was silent, and I had nothing to occupy my thoughts except the loneliness. On the busy shifts, when I would hear the laugh of a guest, which I desired, it reminded me of my father, or smell something, which reminded me of home.

Communication was problematic due to the time difference. When I was able to call home, my family was asleep. At the time they were awake and in their daily activities, I was in the shift area and could not respond. The communications between us had turned into these short, unsatisfactory exchanges of how are you and everything is alright, each of us being unwilling to tell the other the whole truth.

I missed important moments. The graduation of my younger brother. My grandmother's birthday. A friend's wedding. The fact that each of the events I missed was a sort of minor betrayal, a reminder of the cost I was incurring by being here. My family would also post photos and videos, and I would look at them in my room all by myself, and the distance would seem to be a physical hurt to my heart.

This was worst when something difficult occurred at home, and I was not able to be there. And when my mom was ill, all I heard was a shabby phone connection and her weak voice thousands of miles away. In situations where my father required assistance with something, and I was unable to offer it. The regret of not being there, the decision I made, and the choice would torment me during such times.

Being employed as one of the few foreign workers was in itself a challenge. The vast majority of colleagues were nice, yet there was a point where we collided due to the difference in culture. The misunderstandings that appeared insignificant, but when you were already struggling to prove yourself, they felt like a big deal.

One of the times was when I was written up on something that I had not clearly comprehended as wrong. This policy was covered in training, but I overlooked a very important part in the on-demand delivery. I was ashamed to admit that my face blushed when my manager called me in to talk about it. I attempted to clarify, but it went the wrong way round, and I appeared to have been trying to excuse myself instead of trying to gain clarity.

Other colleagues were bitter that H2B workers were even introduced. They viewed us as taking the jobs of the locals, even though we were only employed when locals were not in a position to be used. I noticed remarks, spoken, even whispered, though very loud, in my presence. "They should hire Americans." These are foreign workers who do not know how we do things here. I do not understand why they cannot speak good English.

The comments were little cuts, and at the same time, these little cuts would add up. I began to question myself on all I did, and I was so conscious of my image being taken. I went out of my way, I kept late hours, I did all the shifts that nobody liked, trying to show them that I was worthy to be here, attempting to demonstrate that I was not merely a foreign employee who was occupying a vacancy.

Conflicts also came as a result of mere exhaustion and stress. Due to the busiest moments, there would be tension and no patience. The misunderstanding with the kitchen would end in an argument. Some workmates would bark at me over some petty issue, and their anger regarding the total workload was getting an easy release. I was taught how to keep my head low, apologize even when I was not certain what I was doing wrong, and humble myself instead of being defensive.

It was the pressure to soldier on, internal and external, which was there throughout. Before my departure, I had made promises. To my family, this sacrifice would result in something improved. To me, that I had the strength to take it, whatever it was. Such promises were a burden I had to bear with the homesickness and tiredness.

On the nights, I wondered about everything when I lay in bed and asked myself whether it was worth it. Was the money that I was sending home worth the loss of all that life? Whether the experience that I was getting was worth the cost of loneliness and isolation that I was suffering. During these dark times, the only thing that kept me going was the fact that I could not go home early, as it would be a sign of surrendering to defeat. It would have been worth nothing to have better in all the sacrifices to that point.

So I got up every morning. I put on my uniform. I smiled in the mirror. I said that that was just a transitional phase, every shift took me a step nearer to the expiry of the season, that I was creating something, although I could not see what.

H2B worker experience is not an easy one. It takes away all that one knew and was used to, and you have to recreate yourself in a new location with new regulations. It is a test of all your assumptions about your own strength and resilience. It makes you aware of how far you are ready to go to have an opportunity to have something better.

Chapter 4: Light Through the Cracks

It was not a struggle all the time. Amidst the long shifts and the homesickness, between the cultural adaptation and the physical fatigue, there were some moments of pure joy. There were times when I was reminded of the reasons I had come here in the first place, and why, notwithstanding all that, I was happy to get the chance.

It was these that I would write home about. The things I would say that made my family smile and not worry. The events that made this process not only survive but something meaningful. It is a chapter about such moments, the best that made the difficulties worth it, and the memories that I will keep with me all my life.

In the hospitality industry, you get to meet hundreds of people, and most of them are gone in a few seconds, in the duration of one meal. But some guests make lasting impressions long after they have left. They no longer view you as a mere waiter, but a human being. And in those communications, you recall what it is like to be actually observed.

It had an elderly couple who were now regulars at Marker 36. They asked me to tell them my section each time they came, so in the course of the season, I heard their story. They had forty-seven years together, and they had travelled a lot, but they collected experiences rather than objects. As soon as they discovered that I was a foreigner, they did not ask any polite questions; they were really interested in knowing about my home, my culture, why I came to this country, etc.

The husband himself had worked overseas when he was young, and he knew the kind of loneliness being out of the home can be. One evening when I was missing my home the most, he said. "It gets easier. And whatever you are being taught now, about resilience and adaptability, no one could ever take that out of you." He also told me that his now wife would leave him a big tip every time with a handwritten compliment: "Thank you so well done, your beautiful smile and your excellent service." Etc.

A family with young children had come to Marker 36 on what had been a particularly difficult day for me. I had slept only three hours, was fighting a headache, and felt so homesick I could barely stand.

But the children were so full of life and joy that you couldn't help but be lifted by them. The youngest, maybe four years old, insisted on drawing me a picture. It was a crayon masterpiece of what she said was the "best waiter in the world," with a lopsided smile and a tray holding colorful circles, which I assumed were plates.

I kept that drawing. I always kept it in my wallet neatly, and on the worst days, I would take it out and remind myself that even small gestures can have the greatest repercussions.

Then the businessman was working on his laptop at lunchtime alone at Dockside Bar. He arrived a few days in a row, and we gave each other a few words on duller occasions. He enquired what my goals were, what I had planned to do after the season. He did not nod politely when I told him that I was trying to save money and do all I could know about the restaurant industry. He provided me with tips regarding career advancement, networking, and how to think strategically about what I would like to do in the future.

It was on his final day that he gave me his business card and said, You have something special; you love people, and you are attentive to details. Don't lose that." I never wrote to him, but the fact that there was somebody successful who saw something good in me kept me going on the hard days to come.

You form a new family when you are not at home, and your new family is composed of whoever is ready to stand by you. That was pretty much what happened with some of my colleagues as they became my family in a foreign country.

Another foreign worker who knew the homesickness without requiring me to elaborate on the same was Maria, who was another international worker with a different nationality. During break times, we would sit together with the respective foodstuffs that we had prepared in our small kitchen setups. We didn't need to talk much. Sitting and just sharing food and eating the same kind of food was sufficient to make us both feel a bit less isolated.

James was a neighborhood lad who had served his entire life in restaurants. The first week he adopted me, and I learned his shortcuts and tricks which had never been in a training book. Watch the table body language, he says, watch it. You know what people want even before they come to you. He taught me how to put several tables on my hands without losing my head, how to deal with bad guests gracefully, and how to endear the kitchen staff to me (never forget that you should always say thank you, and you should bring them water in a rush).

The most important thing I liked about James was the fact that he never made me feel less competent due to my learning. He was respectful to my questions, and he rejoiced at my progress. The first time that I managed to cope with one of the most difficult top ten tables all alone, he gave me a high-five in the server station with true pride. "You are no longer a rookie," he said, smiling.

Then there were the kitchen crew- a very heterogeneous group of individuals with diverse backgrounds who worked within the high-pressure, hot climate of the kitchen. They even bothered to know my name (which not everybody did), and they kept a watch on me. In instances where I would do something wrong on an order, they would correct me without making me feel dumb. On the occasions when I decided not to cope with a shift that was difficult, they would bring out a basket of fries or a snack to maintain my energy levels.

Miguel, the head chef, was especially good. Even though he was from a different country and had clawed his way to the top in fifteen years, I believe that he saw in me a younger version of himself. "Every season," he said to me one night as we were closing. "You believe you are only learning to serve food, but you are learning how to deal under pressure, how to resolve issues, how to deal with every type of person. Those skills? They will wait on you everywhere."

Some working days were not just routine but real experiences. Days that helped me not forget that hospitality in its purest form is all about bringing happiness to people.

There was an unexpected and unforgettable moment at Marker 36. The boyfriend had coordinated everything with us in advance and specifically requested a waterfront table at sunset. We carefully arranged it with fresh flowers, had champagne ready on ice, and prepared a special dessert with "Will you marry me?" written in chocolate.

As the sun dipped below the horizon, he asked the question — and when she said yes, the entire restaurant burst into applause. In that instant, strangers became part of their story, sharing in their joy. I felt deeply proud to have played even a small role in one of the most significant days of their lives.

At Marker 36, we celebrated the ninetieth birthday party of a woman. Three generations of her family had come together in a big party, and the stories they told, the laughs they shared, heated the room up. She had tears in her eyes when we took out her cake and sang happy birthday.

I never imagined I would live to ninety, and I certainly never thought I would witness something so beautiful unfolding right in front of me. When I was serving that table, I was not thinking about tips or long hours. I was reflecting on the fact that I was so lucky to be able to experience this tender family moment.

It was something special every time there was a live music night in Dockside Bar. It seems like magic when there is good music, cold drinks, and people having fun.

There was a different energy on such nights. Visitors extended their visits, chatted, and laughed. They would lean further as well, but more to the point, they would reach us as individuals. Dancing would come out of the blue. Conversations would flow. The barrier that exists between server and served would be relaxed.

I recall one evening when we were completely packed to the brim - all the tables were occupied, there was a wait list outside the door, and orders were dashing around. It was the type of disorder that would shatter you. Nevertheless, the band was playing, the guests were waiting, but happy, and this beat that my coworkers and I found that we could all understand. We danced around in a well-choreographed dance, each having needs to fulfill, and we helped each other without consulting one another. At the end of the night, after we had tallied our tips, we were tired and exhilarated. We had lived through the storm, and we had done it in a good way.

Pelican Bay was more than my place of work; it was a place I found beauty at the least unlikely of times. Peace was found in the natural environment, which seemed like a lot when all that was going on seemed to be too much.

The morning shifts possessed a secret: The morning before many people would get up, I would be there to see the sun rise in the water. The heavens would change to dark purple, then pink, then gold, and the water would reflect all the colors. Birds would begin their day, to their calling all that there should be. During the dead time before the stampede started, I would go outside, serve a cup of coffee, and breathe. Just be. Those moments grounded me.

The mangroves surrounding our place were my refuge when I had some breaks. To me, those curved roots and stagnant water were restful. I would stroll there in between shifts of fifteen minutes, and I could sit somewhere and watch the water, the birds, and the inexhaustible green. It helped me remember that there was a world outside the restaurant, outside the problems, outside my minor problems. It made me remember that nature is indifferent to your problems, and it is weirdly reassuring.

There were dolphins now and then, and they just darted out of the bay in the water, and their water-cutters were dashing through it. The last time I met them was when I shouted at a colleague, pointing so much. She smiled at my enthusiasm. "They're here a lot," she said. "You'll get used to it." But I never did. Each time I saw something, it felt as though I was receiving a gift, a means of remembering that I was living in an amazing place, though I could forget it.

The sunsets were magic. When I worked late shifts, I would get out as the sun was setting, and I would see the sky grow orange to red. I would take pictures to send home, try to embrace the beauty of everything, knowing that the camera cannot possibly do the same justice. I would caption them "Look where I am," Look at this place where I am to make my makeshift home.

The friendships that I have made in this season were made in the fire of the common experience. You get attached to people so fast and so fiercely when you have to work with them, even on the worst and the happiest days, when you meet them at their worst and their very best.

Our group of international workers was there, five of them, all of varying nationalities, and all facing the same issues. We became inseparable. During our few days off, we would go out together, and we would take the bus to the local attractions or beaches. We would record all these with photos and laughs. We would cook together and share money and our cooking experience to come up with fusion dishes that were likely to break all rules of traditional cooking, but were a welcome home.

We did not judge each other in our struggles. The other members would come to the rescue when one of us was really having a very difficult day. We would sit with one of us when they got some bad news at home and give them the comfort we could give. Whenever one of us scored a point, a huge tip, praise from a boss, or the achievement of a goal, we celebrated as though it were our whole team's win.

Such friendships were beyond the workplace. We had made each other emergency contacts, those we would call at two in the morning when we felt too homesick or when we needed somebody to talk to. We were the support systems to one another in a place where we neither had any family, nor any history, nor any roots.

There were the local friends too—people who had grown up in the area and who took it upon themselves to help us navigate not just the job but life in America. They would drive us to grocery stores, explain cultural references we didn't understand, and invite us to their homes for holidays when we would otherwise be alone. Their generosity reminded me that kindness exists everywhere, if you're open to receiving it.

What I didn't realize as I was living these moments was that they were changing me. Each positive interaction, each beautiful sunset, each friendship formed—they were building something inside me. Confidence. Resilience. A broader perspective on the world and my place in it.

I was learning that people are fundamentally the same everywhere. They want to be seen, heard, and treated with kindness. They want good food and good company. They want their special occasions to feel special. These universal truths transcended culture, language, and background.

I was learning that joy and hardship can coexist. That you can be homesick and grateful simultaneously. That you can be exhausted and fulfilled at the same time. Life isn't a binary of good or bad—it's a complex mixture of both, and learning to hold that complexity is part of growing up.

The highlights of this season weren't just pleasant memories to look back on. They were proof that I had made the right choice. That this journey, as difficult as it was, was worth it. They were fuel for the harder days, evidence that beauty and connection and meaning could be found even in the most unlikely circumstances.

When people ask me about my time working abroad, these are the stories I tell first. Not because the challenges weren't real or important, but because these moments of light are what made the darkness bearable. They are what transformed a job into an experience, a season into a chapter of my life that shaped who I would become.

Every guest who treated me with dignity, every coworker who became a friend, every sunset that took my breath away, every moment of laughter that cut through the exhaustion—they all reminded me of something essential: I was exactly where I needed to be, learning exactly what I needed to learn, becoming exactly who I needed to become.

The highlights weren't just the peaks between valleys. They were proof that the climb was worthwhile.

Chapter 5: Becoming

When I was new in the service, I believed that the job was to receive orders and deliver food. I was completely wrong. The task was that of reading people, pre-empting what they required, reading the temperament at a table, adjusting my demeanor to the energy levels.

I got to know how to read body language as a language in itself. Crossed arms and no eye contact indicated that they wanted no company- take the order, bring the food, and make minimal checks. To the extent that they were bending forward, eye contact, inquiring about them, they wanted to be engaged, conversed with, and be recommended. And a couple sitting silently staring away at one another demanded space. A couple that had their hands across the table required me to make their evening something special.

I got to know how to differentiate between various types of challenging guests. There were hard ones, because they were in a bad mood, and all that was needed was for one to be tolerant. There were also the hard ones, as they had exceptionally high standards and required me to surpass them. Some were hard because they were difficult by nature, and I would never please them. With these I found I had to do my work as a business and not as personal.

I also got to know how to anticipate needs. The customer table containing young children would require crayons and a children's menu at once. The corporate lunch would require efficiency, no chit-chat, fast delivery, and the bill being paid before they requested. The tourists would be seeking recommendations, tales about the area, and a guide to enable them to make the best out of their experience. The regulars would feel like having their order of things recalled, a stake in pleasant conversation, and the ease of familiarity.

These were the skills of reading people, adapting, and anticipating; they went way beyond the restaurant. I was found using them in all the interactions. I would be able to enter a room and feel the atmosphere. I would be able to maneuver through any people. I was able to make people feel comfortable even in times when I was nervous myself. They were not the skills that could be taught in a book. They had merely grown that way, by experience, by observation, by attending to, by caring to know.

Before this experience, I knew about stress. I didn't. Stress is the second shift with just three hours of sleep, and you have a headache that you cannot shake because you cannot call in sick. Stress will be working with seven tables at once, and the kitchen is already congested, and the guests are becoming impatient. Dealing with a guest who is yelling at you over something that isn't your fault, while you're expected to smile and apologize because it's part of your job, is incredibly stressful.

However, in the course of learning how to cope with the stress, I gained something priceless: real resilience. Not the resilience that one feels after reading inspirational quotes, but the sort of resilience that is a result of taking a beating and putting yourself back on your feet, with each hit, until you realize that you are capable of a lot more than you used to imagine.

I was taught how to remain composed at times of complete disarray. When orders were being mixed up, and guests were complaining, and my manager was miffed, and I felt like crying- I knew how to take a breath, focus, and do one thing at a time. I came to know that everything is made worse when panic sets in, yet calm competence will help in salvaging almost any situation.

I also learnt how to recover. During the early season, I would sit and ponder over the mistakes, and keep on re-experiencing it in my mind, and I believed I had messed everything up. Slowly, I was able to start admitting the mistake, working on what was possible to do, apologising, and going on. I also got to know that everybody commits mistakes, and it is the way you deal with them.

I was taught to drive through a lack of energy. Nighttime, there were days and nights when I was so fatigued that I could hardly contemplate, when my body was screaming for sleep, when each foot pained. Nevertheless, the change was not complete, and the work had to be accomplished, which meant that I discovered some sources of energy that I had not imagined were present in me. I also came to know that the mind quits way before the body, and that at times, one needs to say to the mind that you have one more hour, one more table, one more task to get to the finish line.

This strength became my best asset. It implied that in any field of life going forward, the struggle will never seem as daunting. I possessed evidence of my ability to withstand tough situations. I had a demonstration of the fact that I was stronger than I believed.

The language barrier, which appeared to be too sturdy at the start of the season, was getting less and less important. Not that my English was made perfect, as it was not, but that I was taught that communication is a lot more than words.

I was taught to communicate using tone and body language. True smiling and open posture would translate into friendliness even as I uttered stilted words. Respect may be expressed in eye contact and listening attentively when I could not tell every word that was being spoken. I was taught that it takes better people to react to your way of making them feel rather than the grammar.

I was taught to pose clarifying questions without embarrassment. At a young age, I would deceive myself into thinking I knew something when I did not, and I would end up being wrong and confused. At some point, I came to understand that saying, "Could you please repeat that?" or "Just to make sure I understood correctly…" was not a sign of weakness. It was professionalism. Making sure guests received exactly what they ordered mattered far more than proving I could speak perfect English.

I got to know the vocabulary and regional slang of the industry. I was taught that 86 was a way of telling that we were short. I noticed how the term in the weeds can be used when one of my colleagues was in a difficult situation. I was informed about the distinction between rare and medium-rare and how serious Americans were about their steak temperatures. I was educated about what sweet tea was and why sometimes bless your heart was not as a compliment as it sounded.

However, more to the point, I did learn how to interact with individuals who did not speak my language, that is, not only English as opposed to my mother tongue but also not only Chinese as opposed to English. I also learnt to interact with the elderly couple that had been frequenting the same restaurant for two decades. With the adolescent children who appeared to have their own language altogether. The New Yorker in business, the Midwest family, and the European tourists. The groups possessed their own communication style, and I got to learn to fit in with all of them.

This flexibility, the ability to establish contact with any person, irrespective of their origin or the language of communication, became one of my strongest points.

The technical skills that I acquired were multiple and useful. I also learned how to work multiple tasks at once, which I had never imagined I would ever do, and that entailed taking a customer order. In my mind, I had to keep up with which one of my other tables was to be serviced, what was being served out of the kitchen, and what I had to replenish. I also got to know how to work effectively under time pressure, how to prioritize things, and how to manage my section as though it were a small business.

I was taught how to manage money not only by planning my income, but also in terms of using cash and cards correctly, making change in a short time, and sales tracking. The concept of profit margins was taught to me through the way our managers justified the urge to push some items. The reason is that I got to know about inventory and waste management through observing the operations of the restaurant.

Teamwork is the issue that I learned in a manner that could not be taught by any team-building exercise. When you are there in the trenches with them during a terrible dinner rush, you learn to know what your colleagues need, to interfere without being requested, and to help one another when one is undergoing a difficult situation. You hear that it does not matter as an individual succeeds, but the failure of the team. You know how to celebrate the success of other individuals because you are certain they will celebrate yours.

I got to know about the best customer care. How to transform a complaint into a positive experience. How to exceed expectations. The way to make moments that the guests would recall and discuss. These were not only skills in restaurants, but each of them was a life skill that you will use in any job, any interaction, and any situation that you have to deal with other human beings.

I learned problem-solving. Whenever something went wrong- which it always was going wrong- I was taught to improvise and to be creative in my thinking, to make decisions based on limited information. I also got to know that there is nearly always a solution, provided one remains calm and considers one's options.

Outside the physical abilities, there were also developments in me which were not as measurable, yet may have been even more important.

I became more confident. Not boastfully, but in a silent, substantial manner. I was aware that I was able to cope with hard circumstances as I had already demonstrated it to myself on numerous occasions. I was sure that I would be able to fit in new settings since I was living evidence. I was aware that I could live to be uncomfortable since I did that day by day.

I became more empathetic. Service work presents you with people at their finest and worst. You can see the parent who is stressed and is struggling to have a meal with angry children. You can see the couple obviously in a bad stage. You see the one who is eating alone, who only wants someone to chat with them a little. You get to know that everybody is battling battles which you have no idea about, and that your kindness costs you nothing, but everything.

I became more independent. I lacked a family to rely on, a crash pad. In case of a failure, I needed to correct it by myself. This imposed independence made me realize that I could do more than I believed. It also showed me that I should have confidence in myself and make a decision without necessarily involving my cheques, to be self-reliant.

I became more humble. The work humbled me. Mopping up after others, listening to their grievances, needing to swallow my ego over and over again, it took away any entitlement there could have been in me. But it was no shameful modesty. It was a humble down-to-earthness that made me remember that there is no work too low or high, that all work is dignified, that serving others is noble.

I became more grateful. I used to assume a lot before this experience. A home-cooked meal. A day off to spend with my family. The ease of addressing people in my native language. The comfort of deciphering the cultural allusions. The comfort of the home environment. I am very grateful for these things now. I liked all the goodwill extended to me. Every moment of beauty. Every small victory.

Considering what I have learned in a nutshell, the main lessons would include:

Comfort is overrated. The development occurs out of your comfort zone. Any minute of suffering at this time of the year was the occasion to be made stronger, more competent, more resistant. Applying the principle of not accepting challenges just because they are uncomfortable is a lesson I will never forget in my life.

You can do more than you believe. When I first arrived, I was not sure that I would be able to cope with the job, the time, and the distance to my home. But I did handle it. I lived and even prospered. I now realize that I can do more when I believe that I have exhausted my limits.

Minor gestures count so much. The colleague who was patient with me during my learning time. The guest who treated me with respect when others did not. The friend who had to sit with me when I was homesick. These simple gestures helped me during the most difficult moments. I will do that onward, and I will be nice to the struggling people, as I understand how important it is.

Perspective is everything. Even the worst days as a table server were still better than the best days of many people. I had food, shelter, and opportunity. I was young and healthy and creating a future. It was all bearable learning how to keep perspective; to see the big picture during hard times.

Sacrifice is only meaningful if you extract value from it. I was sacrificing time with my family, comfort, and ease. That sacrifice would be wasted if I didn't grow from it. So I made sure to learn from every experience, to extract every lesson, to become someone worth the sacrifice my family was making in supporting me from afar.

Your story matters. As an H2B worker, I often felt invisible. Just another server, another foreign worker, another face in a uniform. But my story mattered. My dreams mattered. My growth mattered. I learned not to diminish my own journey just because it didn't fit someone else's definition of success.

Looking at myself now, compared to who I was when this journey began, I see someone transformed. The nervous newcomer has been replaced by someone who walks into work with confidence. The person who was overwhelmed by everything is now the one helping train new workers, passing on the lessons I learned through trial and error.

I'm not finished growing. Each day still brings new challenges, new lessons. But I'm no longer afraid of the challenges. I welcome them because I know they're shaping me into someone stronger, someone better, someone ready for whatever comes next.

This season taught me that growth is uncomfortable. It's messy. It involves failure and fear and moments when you want to give up. But it's also beautiful. It's the process of becoming more fully yourself, of discovering capabilities you didn't know you had, of proving to yourself that you can handle more than you ever imagined.

I came here to work. To earn money. To have an experience. But I'm leaving with so much more. I'm leaving with skills that will serve me in any career. With resilience that will carry me through any difficulty. With confidence that comes from having survived and thrived in a foreign land. With a broader perspective on the world and my place in it.

I'm leaving as a different person than the one who arrived. And that person—the one I'm becoming—is someone I'm proud to be.

The work shaped me. The challenges shaped me. The people shaped me. The experiences shaped me. Every difficult moment was a chisel, carving away who I used to be and revealing who I was meant to become.

This is the gift of the H2B worker experience that nobody talks about. Yes, you earn money. Yes, you gain work experience. But more than that, you gain yourself. You discover who you are when everything familiar is stripped away. You learn what you're made of when tested. You become the person you need to be to handle whatever life throws at you next.

And that growth, that becoming, is worth every sacrifice, every challenge, every moment of homesickness and exhaustion. Because at the end of the season, you don't just go home with money in your pocket. You go home as a transformed version of yourself, carrying lessons and strengths that no one can ever take away.

That is the true value of this journey. Not what I earned, but who I became in the earning of it.

Chapter 6: Reflection

Looking back on my experience as an H2B employee reveals two sides of myself. There's the individual who got off that Miami plane in November 2016, anxious, unsure, carrying one tattered luggage and fantasies bigger than my own could support. And there's the person I am now—one shaped by hardship, tested by distance, and strengthened by every challenge overcome.

The change did not happen overnight. Small events spanning several seasons caused it. It occurred when I discovered how to clean fifteen rooms in one shift at Belhurst Castle. It occurred when I finally felt comfortable approaching a table as a server, not only as a busser. It came as I drove myself to work for the first time, having picked up something I had never dreamed I could master. Every time I opted to remain concentrated instead of giving in to depression, homesickness, or diversion, it occurred.

This trip imparted knowledge no classroom ever could. I developed resilience—not the sort seen in motivational quotes, but rather the kind born of being knocked down and opting to rise back up. I acquired adaptability, which is the capacity to walk into a new job, a new city, a new country, and figure out how to not only survive but also flourish. I discovered the importance of focus—of maintaining my gaze on my objectives despite everything around me tugging me in several directions.

Most importantly, though, I discovered variety. Living and working with people from Hungary, Romania, Mexico, Africa, England, and across the Caribbean taught me that all over, humanity is fundamentally the same. Everyone misses their families. Every one of us has a dream we are pursuing. Every one of us has stories of hope and hardship. The cultural divisions that were first thought to be so great turned into bridges of understanding. Initially, irksome language obstacles showed me that the connection goes past words.

Being ill in a strange country is among the most difficult situations you can encounter. That's when you really grasp the sense of isolation: when you get the flu, and there's no mother to bring you soup, no wife to give you medicine, no family to drive you to the doctor. But it's also when you learn that your family may comprise the people around you, regardless of their background. Your colleagues who drop in on you. Your neighbors who deliver you water. The other H2B employees know exactly what you're going through since they are also going through it.

Food developed into identity instead of just nourishment. Finding Jamaican cuisine in America felt like discovering a fragment of home in an unknown country.

Learning how to use the Uber app to get to the Bravo store was about maintaining my connection to who I was and where I came from rather than merely about transportation. Those meals of yams, breadfruit, plantain—they reminded me that distance does not alter who one is. I always belonged to Jamaica regardless of how many seasons I labored or how well I fit into American society.

The H2B program gave me three years and six seasons to transform. Every season called for me to grow someone fresh without losing myself. Every job, from serving to bussing to housekeeping, instructed me in different skills. But the actual education came from discovering who I could be, not from service procedures or cleaning methods.

Those days on Block Island in Rhode Island, when there was no phone line, and I couldn't speak to my wife or family, come back to me. The seclusion was killing. Our room had three bunk beds, a toilet, and four men cohabitating in that little area—no kitchen. For a four-minute journey, a taxi costs twenty dollars. Everything costs money. Everything was hard. But summer approached with hordes, labor, and meaning. Always driving myself to the limit, I sometimes worked from seven in the morning until ten at night—sometimes as a beach boy, occasionally as housekeeper.

Those long hours taught me endurance. Not just physical endurance, though, my body also certainly learnt that. However, mental and emotional fortitude—the capacity to keep going when you're weary, homesick, and doubtful if it's all worth it—helps, being able to grin at visitors even though your heart is burdened. The capacity to perform admirably when all inside of you desires to give up.

That was when all the suffering became tangible; I finally got to travel to Jamaica in October and met my kid for the first time at one and a half years old. Holding him, seeing his face, hearing his laugh—it made every difficult moment worth it. That one month at home replenished me for the following season. It brought back to mind my reasons for doing this. It was important, not just for the money. It was worthwhile, not only for the experience, but for him. For my family. With every season, every paycheck, and every lesson learned, I was building something for the future.

Looking back today, I can see how every challenge got me ready for the next one. The language barriers at Pelican Bay helped me to learn to convey beyond words. The physical requirements of housekeeping showed me what my body could tolerate. Rochester's cold and Block Island's loneliness developed my mental toughness. Becoming a server from a busser gave me self-assurance. Each season built another degree of toughness, another skill, another knowledge.

My encounter with variety went beyond getting to know people from other nations. It was about discovering several perspectives on life, several working methods, and several modes of thought. From my Mexican coworkers, I learned about family loyalty. Work-life balance lessons came from my European colleagues. My African acquaintances taught me about persistence. As I created a new short-term family, my Caribbean siblings and sisters made me think of home.

I discovered that cooperation goes beyond a corporate buzzphrase. That's when you learn what teamwork truly is—when you're in the trenches during a dinner rush, orders are backing up, guests are impatient, the kitchen is overworked, and everyone is stressed. It means assisting your colleague even as you yourself are sinking. It means hiding for someone who's having a terrible day, since you know they will cover for you when you need it. Celebrating one another's accomplishments is part of being in this together.

I started a waiter's book to become more astute as the seasons changed. At night, I researched the menu. I rehearsed the steps of service. I forced myself into tournaments and won every time—not because I was competing against others, but rather because I was battling who I was the season before. I began measuring my development against my own prior limitations rather than comparing myself to my colleagues.

A worker who stays focused changes by the end of the season. That was always my goal, not just to get through it, not only to earn the paycheck, but to leave better than I arrived. Growth requires intention. It means becoming someone my family can be proud of, and someone I can be proud of too.

Looking back now on all I have gone through, I see that this path brought me more than I had ever dreamed. Yes, I was compensated. I did, indeed, get employment experience. More still, though, I got myself. When everything I know is gone, I learned who I am. Tested, I came to know what I am composed of. I evolved into the man I had to be to manage whatever life next brought at me.

I want to pass on what I've discovered to anybody thinking about the H2B path or already halfway through it. These ideas are lessons for thriving in the program and employing it as a springboard for the rest of your life; they're not just pointers for surviving it.

Stay Focused

The most crucial counsel I can provide is this. As an H2B worker, stay concentrated. You need to concentrate as you have a family back home. Someone depends on you. You have goals you're pursuing. Every direction provides distraction: loneliness, exhaustion, pressure, missing home, extended hours, unfamiliar surroundings. However, it is the focus that distinguishes surviving a season from developing from it.

Every day starts with a decision. You are weary. Your body hurts. Your thoughts wander back to your family, your nation, the life you put on hold. Staying focused, however, means recalling your purpose for coming. You came not for comfort. You arrived for opportunity—for personal growth, for development, for the shaping of oneself, for a better future.

At the job, focus counts for everything. There is no leeway for error, whether you are running food, welcoming guests, or cleaning a room. A missed item can turn into a grievance. One distracted second might destroy trust. Lock in. Since it does, treat every room, every tray, every table as if it matters.

Additionally, concentrating helps to safeguard your peace. Avoid conflict. Keep off rumors. Living with many people from various cultures can test your patience. Your energy should not be devoted to every argument. Not every idea calls for a reply from you. Safeguard your mental area so you can appear strong the next day.

There will be days when hunger, weariness, and tension strive to split your attention. Days you skip lunch only to fulfill your schedule. Days you stroll to work in bad weather. Days when your phone stays quiet, and home seems impossibly far off. On those days, discipline becomes focus; one keeps working even when enthusiasm is absent.

Let your attention become more precise as you advance through several jobs and seasons. Work after dark. Regular practice will help you hone your talents. Push oneself. Start comparing yourself to who you were the season before, instead of others. The employee who remains concentrated not only ends the season but also changes.

Learn to change yourself.

Survival demands adaptation; it's not a decision on the H2B path. Every season asks you to change while still retaining yourself: new positions, new requirements, new people, new expectations. You quickly realize that as you bid farewell to home, your family, and everything familiar, comfort departs as well.

You have to reset yourself every time you reach a new destination: fresh housing, fresh flatmates, fresh timetable, new work criteria, fresh uniform. Everything seems strange—the food, the weather, the tempo, the way people communicate. Fast learning is required of you. View more and say less. Pay attention closely. Because expectations are great and errors are expensive, learn by watching.

Adaptation at work calls for mastery of many roles. Being a housekeeper teaches speed, discipline, and detail orientation. You learn how to move with pride and intent when you clean fifteen to twenty-three rooms a day. As a busser, you change to urgency—running trays, viewing kitchen displays, moving fast while being accurate. For a server, adaptation means building confidence, speaking clearly, upselling, and handling pressure. As an H2B worker, you must remain alert since all eyes are always fixed on you.

Adaptation also accompanies you home. Being around unknown people from many countries teaches humility and patience. Sharing restricted quarters helps you manage your feelings and value differences. Some nights are noisy—games, music, celebrations that render sleep impossible. Certain nights are solitary. Every circumstance shows you how to adapt without breaching.

There will be times you would prefer not to go to work. On days your body is exhausted, your mind is overworked, and your heart yearns to return home. Still, adaptation is showing up regardless. It is hiking to work in the rain. It implies omitting lunch to complete the project. It means conquering anxiety and acquiring the capacity to perform under duress.

Adaptability is a strength every season. What once felt like a challenge turns commonplace. Once regarded as unachievable, it has become usual. Adapting, you find, helps you to reach your potential rather than lose yourself. You are changed by the trip of the H2B. It helps you to be brave, resilient, and flexible. Every season gets you ready for the next struggle and sharpens you.

Discover Your Food, Discover Your Peace

Missing home is among the most challenging aspects of working as an H2B. Not only the people but also the food. Food has memories with it. Food offers consolation.

Food has character. Leaving your nation means leaving not just your family but also the flavor of home.

There will be days when the isolation hits harder, and all you want is something familiar. For me, it was yams, breadfruit, plantain, a fresh mango from a tree, ripe bananas from a fallen tree, and jelly coconut water. Something that reminded me of my starting point. You are, however, in another nation, and those items are not easy to obtain.

That's when technology becomes a blessing. Download the Uber app. Inquiry helps. Look for shops offering food from your culture. I was looking for the Bravo store selling Jamaican cuisine. I was shocked; I wasn't expecting to find Jamaican food in America, but I did. The Uber program evolved from a simple product. It linked my palate of home with me.

Many H2B employees adjust to Walmart shopping, but occasionally, you can't get your own food there. Finding what you would eat is difficult. You must hence locate your path. Applications to download: Make taxi orders. Wander about to find what you want. Taste something familiar as you enter a store and smell the spices; it quickly alters your mood. You are yourself once more, not just an H2B employee far from home.

That supper brings to mind who you are striving for, why you are working so hard, and where you are returning. Purchasing food from home is more about mental survival than it is about appetite. It's about comfort following a protracted shift. Rewarding yourself follows days of labor. It's about finding your culture once again in a land where everything feels foreign.

On days you cannot communicate with your wife or family, food represents them. It serves as a reminder that distance does not change identity. No matter your job or number of seasons, you never stop belonging to your hometown.

You will also pick up the ability to fit in with new foods and customs. That is part of the process. However, staying connected to your roots helps you to remain balanced, whether you order meals from Amazon, locate ethnic supermarkets, or cook with fellow employees from your country. It helps you get up the following day and repeat everything.

Finding your way can occasionally not come from huge occasions. Sometimes it originates from a delivery bag, hot, familiar, and brimming with home.

Celebrate Variety

One of the most important lessons the H2B path teaches you is how to live with people you never envisioned sharing space with. Diversity follows you home, into your room, into your kitchen, into your silence and your development; it is not only visible at work.

Living and working with individuals from all walks of life—Europe, Mexico, Africa, Central America, the Caribbean—you will be an H2B employee. Varied dialects, cuisine, ideologies, and means of reasoning. Initially, it's unpleasant. You abandon your family, and suddenly, you are among others who have also left their families behind. Everybody has their own narrative, suffering, and hope.

At home, you have a limited area, bedrooms, beds, and bathrooms. Privacy is unusual. One must be patient. You must master how to respect strangers, how to connect even when language is a roadblock, and how to coexist without allowing aggravation to become violence.

Some days will be challenging. Some days will be isolated. Those same days, however, will also help you to develop tolerance, humility, and understanding. Diversity turns into teamwork at work. In the kitchen, on the floor, behind the scenes, everyone relies on one another. Various civilizations have one purpose: get the work finished.

You will discover that perfection has no country of origin. Working hard talks every tongue. There will be occasions when cultural variations result in errors. Sometimes you speak the wrong thing to someone from another country, which leads to disagreement. However, there will also be times of laughter, shared food, music, and difficulties.

People around you—wherever they come from—become your temporary family when you are distant from home. You will run across people who seem like your sister, your brother. When you fall ill, you begin to realize how deeply you miss the care and comfort that once surrounded you, and how much those quiet acts of love truly meant. You have no family to accompany you to the doctor. Being sick abroad is quite difficult.

Your diverse family then has to close and become one. Not only at home, but also at work; not only on the floor; not just as a team player. You can't treat each other like enemies. The H2B experience shows you that heterogeneity is not a drawback but rather a benefit. It helps to shape your character. It shows you how to listen, how to change, and how to go above what you believed you were. It gets you ready for life as well as for employment.

Diversity teaches you resilience. Diversity helps you to grow respect. Diversity lets you come to know who you really are. You study languages you never believed you could speak. You find out what various cuisines taste like. You grasp the worth of several societies. And you evolve into a more whole, more competent, more kind human being through everything.

Protect Your Mental Well-Being

Long hours, difficult assignments, and exhaustion define the physical problems of the H2B job, obviously. However, the mental and emotional hurdles are just as tangible and frequently tougher to negotiate. You struggle in silence with loneliness, homesickness, isolation, worry about family back home—often while putting on a grin for visitors.

One should accept these emotions rather than repress them. Missing your family is love, not weakness. Being human means feeling overwhelmed at times; it does not mean you are failing. The key is not allowing those feelings to control your goals or derail your progress.

Find good outlets when you can, call home even if the talks are brief. Maintain a journal. Exercise. Like those morning sunrises or evening strolls I discovered at Pelican Bay, I search for peaceful times in nature. Reach out to other employees who share your experiences. Make a temporary family that can assist you during difficult times.

Remember that every sacrifice has a timeline. Every season concludes. You're not doing this forever; rather, you're doing this for a goal, for a limited time, to create something better. Keep that attitude when the days seem unending.

Remain Hungry for Growth

Don't merely exist throughout your seasons; let them help you to develop. Every position presents a chance to learn something fresh. Every difficulty presents an opportunity for skill growth. Every challenging manager or tough coworker is imparting lessons on endurance, professionalism, or patience.

Study. Exercising. Force yourself. Refuse to be ordinary. Become the best housekeeper they have ever known if you work for one. If you are a busser, study all you can about service so you might become a server. Learn the menu if you are a server, improve your technique, and create relationships with customers.

Develop knowledge fit for use beyond this position. Managing money. Effective means of communication.

Solving challenges: Working with several types of people. These are lifetime abilities that will help you in whatever you do next, not only restaurant talents.

Construct bridges, not barriers.

Some H2B employees erroneously separate themselves, only to associate with others from their own nation, only to consume their own food, and only to speak their own tongue. I see the consolation in that, yet you are passing over chances.

Develop friendships with every single individual—study from the local employees who are knowledgeable about the system. Get in contact with other foreign workers with your background. Be polite with management as they decide your chances, your references for next jobs, and your schedule. Welcome visitors with sincere warmth; they could remember you, suggest you, or even present you with unexpected chances.

Doors you didn't know existed can be opened by the network you develop throughout your H2B years. The people I encountered throughout my first season enabled me to secure employment in subsequent seasons. Managers who recognized my potential gave me chances for promotion. Connections that counted were those of visitors who enjoyed my service.

Handle Your Money Wisely

Since you are here to make money, be deliberate in how you spend it. Spending is simple to get carried away with: going out with coworkers, purchasing unnecessary goods, and sending too much home without leaving enough for yourself.

Set up a budget. Know precisely how much you are making and where it is going. Though also save for yourself, send money home to help your family. Money will be needed between seasons. You'll need money for catastrophes. When you head back, you will need money to invest in your future.

Recall that every dollar you make came from a sacrifice—long hours, hard effort, time away from family. Show respect for that sacrifice by judiciously employing your cash.

Know Your Rights

You, as an H2B employee, have privileges. You are deserving of fair pay, secure working conditions, and respectful treatment. Because you are foreign or because you require work, don't let anyone exploit you.

Understand your duties at the same time. Follow the guidelines. Come on time. Create excellent work. Honor the program that gave you this opportunity. Your behavior influences how future H2B employees from your nation will be treated.

Remain in Touch with Residence

Technology helps us stay in touch more easily than ever. Make use of it. Make frequent video calls to your loved ones. Photograph sent. Tell us your experiences. Let them join your path even though they cannot be there in person.

Still be truthful about the difficulties with them. Don't act like everything is ideal when it is not. They need to grasp what you are going through so that they may emotionally help you. And so you may be there for them even from afar, you need to know what's going on at home.

Prepare for the Future

The H2B program is temporary. Don't let the present consume you such that you lose sight of the future. When your three years end, what will you do? How will you handle the funds you have accumulated? Which abilities will you carry with you? Which prospects will you chase?

Contemplate these issues as you are still laboring. Link with those who might assist you in the future. Acquire knowledge that applies to many sectors. Save strategically for the company or investment you wish to launch once you get home.

The aim is not only to make it through your H2B seasons. One aims to use them as a springboard for the life you want to create.

Recall Your Reason for Beginning

There will be days you want to give up. Days when you wonder why you ever believed this was a wise move. Times when the homesickness is so intense you can hardly get going—days when everything seems too challenging, too isolated, too overwhelming.

Recall those days when you began. Keep in mind the family you are assisting. Bear in mind the future you are creating. Keep in mind the person you are growing into via this journey. Keep in mind that this sacrifice has a time and a purpose.

I had a photo of my son in my pocket. On the toughest days, I would stare at it and remind myself that every challenging event was bringing me closer to providing him the life he deserves. Find your own interpretation of that—whatever inspires your mission and keeps you going forward.

The H2B path is difficult. Anyone who says differently is lying. It is intellectually challenging, emotionally taxing, and physically strenuous. You will be tested in never-before-imaged ways. It will go past restrictions you were unaware of. It will make you develop whether or not you believe you are ready.

Yet it is among the most treasured experiences you may have. It equips you with fortitude, flexibility, and resiliency. It reveals what you are able to do when pressed to your boundaries. It helps you see other civilizations, points of view, and ways of living. It shapes character in ways no classroom or cozy setting ever could.

Finding your path as an H2B employee doesn't make the road any less challenging. It implies that you develop muscle strength. One day, you will look back and understand you were being created rather than lost. Every difficulty was influencing your development. Every trying period readied you. Every sacrifice was really worthwhile.

Considering the individual who landed in Miami in November 2016 and the person I am today reveals development not otherwise possible. Strength gained via hardship is what I see. I see confidence developed through obstacles. I have a wider view of the earth and my role in it.

To anybody now traveling this path: you are not alone. Thousands of individuals before you have tread this path. Right now, thousands of people are hiking it with you. Many thousands will follow you too. The same difficulties, the same sacrifices, and the same drive to create something better are all shared by us.

Keep attention. Remain disciplined. Never lose your hunger for development. Welcome variety. Safeguard your mental health. construct bridges. Make plans for the future. Above everything, remember why you started.

That employee—the one who remains concentrated, flexible, learns, and develops—does not only end the season. That employee exits the season altered. That employee grows to be someone their family can be proud of. One that they themselves may be proud of.

This trip will alter you. Allow it to improve you. Let it develop you into the person you should be. Let it serve as the basis for the future you're striving so much to build.

And you will have more than just money in your pocket when you at last return home, see your family, hug your children, and greet your loved ones. You will have knowledge nobody can ever take away. Abilities you will use all your life. Strength to overcome any difficulty. And pride in knowing you did something tough, important, meaningful, and significant.

That is the actual worth of the H2B path. Who you grow into while earning it, not what you make.

You showed up for the opportunity. You stayed to develop. You changed.

That is your narrative. Own it. Live it. And use it to construct the future you merit.

Jermaine Andre Howard

THE END